Floodgate

Larry Gelbart

A SAMUEL FRENCH ACTING EDITION

SAMUEL FRENCH

FOUNDED 1830

SAMUELFRENCH.COM
SAMUELFRENCH-LONDON.CO.UK

CHARACTERS

THE VOICE OVER

SENATOR FAIRLY GROSS

SENATOR ORAL PROCTOR

COMMITTEE MEMBERS

SENATOR STILLBOURNE

MICHAEL BROWNIE

LOWELL DICKLER

CONGRESSWOMAN VIRGINIA ALEXANDER

Secretary of the Office for the Security of the Homeland against International Terror and Extremists, **MICHAEL CHERKOFF**

RONALD DUMSFELD

GENERAL RICHARD D. NYER

MR. SIMIAN PANDERGAST

THE VICE PRESIDENT

THE PRESIDENT

THE VOICE OVER. *(C-Spanish)* Having presented past retrospectives of Water, Iran-Contra and Mastergate, AGN, the All Gate Network, is pleased to present highlights of the recent hearings of the Select Joint House and Senate Oversight Committee, which was created to investigate the latest federal failure and subsequent global embarrassment when the perfect storm that hit the nation's capital, already awash in scandal and a cascade of corruption, was hit by a tidal wave of revulsion against the present administration, leaving the city so battered and engulfed it was soon strewn with the body politic, as whole branches of the Federal government were completely swept away. The proceedings, quickly dubbed by the media as "Floodgate," were held at the temporary capital of the United States, which is located in Aurora, Colorado, inside the show ring at the headquarters of the International Arabian Horse Association.

(As the meeting is brought to order in the background with a gavel:) Gavelling the first session to order was the committee's perpetual chairman, Senator Fairly Gross. Senator Gross is perhaps best known as the co-author, along with Idaho Senator Warren Negligence, of the Gross-Negligence Bill. The legislation, which took effect last Mother's Day, calls for the mandatory deportation of all undocumented newborns, following arthroscopic fingerprinting of any suspected illegal embryos.

(sound: A gavel)

THE VOICE OVER. Here then, is Senator Gross.

GROSS. Good morning, ladies and gentlemen, and welcome to these hearings to investigate the course of events as well as the aftermath which followed in its

GROSS. *(cont.)* wake. Let me state at the start of this onset that, speaking on the bequest of this committee that we will not be satisfied until we have a complete understanding of what it is that precisely went so wrong during the cataclysmical events of the date that will forever be heretofore immortalized as Eleven-Nine. A second committee, charged with investigating everything that went right on that date in time will meet later this morning at twelve, and will remain in session if necessary until just after lunch. These hearings, if they do nothing else, will carry with them a message that is meant to reverberate far beyond the mere shores of Colorado. It is a message to the world that no single event, however ruinous - no single occurence however devastating - will ever be catastrophical enough to deter these United States of America from committing ourselves to the next. I am especially, both Senate and House-proud, at the bipartisan intrastructure of this committee, a fact which is no better exemplafied than by the appointment of this committee's co-chair - one of my oldest and most ranking friends - Senator Oral Proctor. Senator Proctor?

PROCTOR. Thank you, Mister Chairman.

THE VOICE OVER. Senator Oral Proctor, an old Washington hand, has served for thirty consecutive terms in the U.S. Senate, including the fifteen years he spent while doing ten-to-twenty.

PROCTOR. I am, as always, grateful for the warmth of the chair.

GROSS. As am I yours, sir.

PROCTOR. Allow me to say how forward looking I am to the senator's distinguished hand upon the keel of the bipartisanship that will required in this inquiry into the reasons for the recent abandonment of the city of Washington, D.C., in the former District of Columbia of itself.

PROCTOR. For a majority of those of us in the minority, these hearings will hopefully allow us to finally connect all our dots in a row – Above all, they will offer the nation the opportunity to learn at long last from the chief executive himself, the question he has so standfastly refused to answer to this day. Namely: "What did the president know? And when did the vice president tell him it was all right that he finally could?" Surely it is time that this unseemly and seemingly unheeded question receive whatever attention the American people may still have the necessary span for.

GROSS. Not to cut the distinguished gentleman off in midharangue, but as it happens, the Chair is in receipt of a response to our most recent request, which was sent to the temporary Oval Trailer, and is signed by the president himself of these United States.

PROCTOR. Do I understand, Mister Chairman, that the President has finally deigned up and written the committee?

GROSS. He has.

PROCTOR. And why, may I ask, was I not told of this?

GROSS. This is that actually telling of it, sir. Farther to the point, the president states that, rather than continuing to decline our repeated invitations to testify, he has decided to provide us with as many answers as it may take in order to truthfully answer any of the questions which we might see fit to pose.

(The news causes a stir among the **COMMITTEE MEMBERS.***)*

STILLBOURNE. Mister Chairman?

GROSS. Senator Stillbourne?

STILLBOURNE. Do I understand, Mister Chairman, that the president has actually agreed to appear before the members of this committee?

GROSS. If I may quote from one of the passages in his letter which he wrote that someone else wrote.

(reads:) "In the interest of creating the kind of transparency that you can see through, let me say that I am in

GROSS. *(cont.)* complete agreement with what I have repeatedly said so many times before, and that is that there is no way that things can ever go forward unless someone finally gets to the bottoms of them. "It is toward those ends that I hope finally to begin." I would hope that answers the gentleman's question?

STILLBOURNE. And did the president happen to say that in his appearing before us that such an appearance would be one that he intends making in person?

GROSS. It is my assumption that in his appearance he will be as in person as he can be.

STILLBOURNE. Here, in this chamber? Not pre-taped?

GROSS. In real time, I would also assume.

STILLBOURNE. I think it's been pretty well established by now that what is real for this president is not necessarily what is real for anyone else.

PROCTOR. Has the Chair been informed as to what, if any, the ground rules might be regarding such a presidential appearance? We would not be the first investigative committee to be stonewalled by the claims of executive privilege that are so frequently claimed by so many of our privileged executives.

GROSS. The president did have one provision, provisowise.

PROCTOR. And that is?

GROSS. That he be allowed to appear before us accompanied by the vice president.

STILLBOURNE. The vice president?

GROSS. That is what he intimidated, yes.

(Another bit of murmuring from **THE COMMITTEE.***)*

STILLBOURNE. Apparently the White House – ?

(A gavel halts the murmuring.)

GROSS. Senator Stillbourne?

STILLBOURNE. Apparently the White House is still willing to add to the impression that whereas most vice presidents are content to remain in the shadows, what we have is a White House in which the shadow continues to throw the image of the president.

GROSS. I would remind my learned colleague that what the president thinks is certainly not for me to say.

STILLBOURNE. Both those jobs belonging exclusively to the vice president, of course?

(Again, there is murmuring from **THE COMMITTEE.***)*

(sound: the gavel.)

THE VOICE OVER. The opening acrimonies concluded, the chairman turned his attention to the questionable portion of the hearings.

GROSS. Is the first witness present for the purpose of being sworn?

BROWNIE. I am, Mister Chairman.

GROSS. You are Michael Brownie?

BROWNIE. In terms of my name, that is who I am, yes, sir.

GROSS. If you'd please raise your right hand?

DICKLER. Point of order, Your Chairmanship?

GROSS. You being exactly who, if you would be so good?

DICKLER. I am Lowell Dickler, Mister Chairman. I am a member of the law firm of Redd, White and Blau.

GROSS. And the exact nature of your purpose is what, sir?

DICKLER. I am acting as outside counsel attorney for Mister Brownie.

GROSS. And just what is it you'd like to act out, Mister Dickler?

DICKLER. In any way that I can, Mister Chairman. Starting, if I may, on the matter of the swearing in of the witness himself, sir.

GROSS. Counsel has some problem with that?

DICKLER. If it please the Chair, having been administered a lifelong oath at the moment of his birth, Mister Brownie is in fact pre-sworn-in for this and any and all other investigative hearings at which he might ever and no doubt will continue to find himself before.

GROSS. You were sworn in when you were born, Mister Brownie, do I understand that correctly?

BROWNIE. Each time that I was, yes, sir.

GROSS. You have, as seems to be the rage du jour, been born more than once, is that the drift of your gist?

BROWNIE. In point of fact, I have, Mister Chairman.

GROSS. The second time for you being the charm?

BROWNIE. The third, more actually.

GROSS. Your third birth?

BROWNIE. I am a born again born again, yes, sir.

GROSS. Practice makes perfect, is that the idea?

BROWNIE. I can only pray that it does, yes, sir.

DICKLER. I would point out to the committee that Mister Brownie is a graduate of the Rob Jones University, Mister Chairman.

GROSS. The Rob Jones University in New Testament, New Mexico?

BROWNIE. Yes, sir. I was lucky enough to receive a four year Rapture Scholarship.

DICKLER. The witness was a bit of a religious prodigy, Mister Chairman.

GROSS. Apparently.

DICKLER. He was on his knees at the age of two.

GROSS. I see Mister Brown attended Rob Jones High, Rob Jones Elementary, Rob Jones K, and Pre-K?

BROWNIE. Yes, sir.

GROSS. Pre-K and Pre-Pre-K?

BROWNIE. Jesus' Fetuses, yes, sir.

GROSS. Very good. Mister Brownie, the committee is hoping that you might give us some idea of why it is we seem to have no idea of why it is we seem to have no idea of why –

DICKLER. Mister Chairman, if I may, for the purpose of interrupting you –

GROSS. Mister Dickler?

DICKLER. Mister Chairman, Mister Brownie would like to make a short, opening statement, sir, after which he is prepared to answer any of your questions that to the best of his ability to recollect he might or might not be able to recall.

GROSS. The Chair will table that request for the moment, my experience being that, while short statements come and rarely ever go, it's never too late to make an opening one.

DICKLER. I thank the Chair.

GROSS. For the record, Mister Brownie, you are, at this particular frame in time, a member of the current administration?

BROWNIE. I have the honor to serve at the P-Double-O-P, sir.

GROSS. The POOP?

BROWNIE. At the pleasure of our president, sir.

GROSS. And in what way do you find yourself pleasuring him?

BROWNIE. My status at this time in the present is somewhat fluxed up, sir, being as I am presently in the process of resigning my current position, my resignation being delayed so that it can be synchronously timed to coincide with my future firing.

GROSS. Which position will then have become your former what?

BROWNIE. The one I presently hold now? Is that what you're asking?

GROSS. If memory serves, I believe so, yes.

BROWNIE. I am the soon-to-be ex-Director of the Critical Organizational and Management Agency, sir.

GROSS. The agency we know as COMA.

BROWNIE. COMA are us, yes, sir.

GROSS. And it was under your watch that that agency was charged with responding to the massive damage done to the capital during Eleven-Nine?

BROWNIE. From everything that I've read about me, that would appear to be true, yes, sir.

GROSS. COMA would, of course, have kept detailed files of its comings and possibly tardy goings, as well as a timeline of all matters of any import related to the debacle?

BROWNIE. Having learned that every disaster is a rehearsal for a hearing, I actuated every facet of my agency's technology, sir, for the purpose of recording and preserving up to the minutest of each day's calamitous events.

GROSS. And in your deposition you pledged to make those records available to this committee, did you not?

BROWNIE. I so did, yes, sir.

GROSS. And will you now make good on that pledge, Mister Brownie?

BROWNIE. I'm afraid, sir, that as much as I like keeping my word as often as possible, I won't be able to do that, sir.

GROSS. You will not?

BROWNIE. No, sir. Due to budgetary trims, Mister Chairman, trims which were based on the projection of more additional funds that were deemed would prove necessary in order to cope with future disasters, COMA's security system was switched from our state-of-the-art satellite and interplanetary surveillance system to the more economical use of German Shepherds.

GROSS. German Shepherds? Dogs?

BROWNIE. Dogs, sir, yes, sir.

GROSS. You went from human to canine intelligence?

BROWNIE. We did, yes, sir.

GROSS. And the result of this change?

BROWNIE. The dogs ate my records, sir.

GROSS. All of them?

BROWNIE. Every jot and dittle, yes, sir.

DICKLER. Fortunately, we have the president's word for it that, under Mister Brownie's command, COMA did do a heck of a job.

BROWNIE. Immodesty aside, I must say the I agree with the president's appraisal of my rating, Mister Chairman. I, too, believe Eleven-Nine was perhaps the finest rescue and recovery operation with which I have ever found myself connected to.

GROSS. Senator Proctor? Would you like to question the witness?

PROCTOR. Thank you, Mister Chairman. In truth, I believe I already do. Good morning, Mister Brownie.

(a pause, then)

Good morning, sir.

(after another pause)

Let the record show, Mister Chairman, that although he was greeted twice, the witness chose to remain silent and uncooperative.

DICKLER. As the Chair well knows, Mister Chairman, the witness has previously been most forthcoming, insomuch as he has already testified under oath regarding the goodness of this morning, sir.

GROSS. And the witness is content to stand on his previous response?

DICKLER. Without prejudicing either his civil, publication, or motion picture rights, the witness has no desire to rescind, redact, or recuse any part of his testimony in the matter of this particular morning in time, Mister Chairman.

PROCTOR. I thank the counselor for keeping his answer down to a simple obfuscation. Now then, the flood, Mister Brownie, and the subsequent chaos that flowed on the heels of it.

BROWNIE. Yes, sir?

PROCTOR. That was perhaps your finest rescue and recovery operation? That is how you would characterize your performance?

BROWNIE. I was in fact quoting the President of the United States, Senator. Those were his very own words that he muttered.

PROCTOR. The president's own words?

BROWNIE. Reading those inscribed on the back of the Freedom Medal, sir. The one he presented me in recognition of my disastrous services.

PROCTOR. Can you understand, Mister Brownie, that a good many people find it obscene to reward, to laud the perpetrators of such shoddy work? That any action that honors inaction degrades those honors to a degree that borders on the farcical?

BROWNIE. There's no pleasing everyone, Senator. I don't think I have ever been able to please a single soul in my entire life. Starting with my own parents, who were arrested in the maternity ward for trying to unplug my incubator.

PROCTOR. That is, perhaps a bit more than anyone really needs to know.

BROWNIE. Tell me about it.

PROCTOR. Maybe we might be able to glean a bit of insight if we try to fathom out why you happened to be chosen by the president of the United States to head up COMA in the first place.

BROWNIE. I'm always happy to help with the gleaning, sir.

PROCTOR. The president must have had something in mind when he chose to appoint you, wouldn't you say so?

BROWNIE. I'm not sure the president can ever be said to have anything at all on his mind, Senator. Being president's difficult enough for him, without throwing in a whole lot of thinking.

PROCTOR. Well, let's say that he did have something in mind.

BROWNIE. A hypothetical.

PROCTOR. In what work of a previous nature had you been engaged to that might have convinced anyone with half a mind that you had the capability of running the largest emergency relief agency in the world?

BROWNIE. What was I doing priorly?

PROCTOR. In that manner of speaking, yes.

BROWNIE. At the time of my appointment, sir, I had been located in D.C. as a member of the wine and spirits industry.

PROCTOR. The manufacture of wine and spirits?

BROWNIE. The distribution of them.

PROCTOR. Their distribution?

BROWNIE. The delivery of them, sir.

PROCTOR. You delivered alcohol, is that what I'm hearing?

BROWNIE. You might say I took the fifth all over town, yes, sir. I delivered liquor to the Pentagon. I delivered liquor to the cabinet.

PROCTOR. And was the White House one of your regular stops, as well?

BROWNIE. Most of those orders, Senator - gin and vodka, mostly – most of those I had orders to first transfer into Evian water bottles.

PROCTOR. Humble enough beginnings, wouldn't you say, Mister Brownie, for a man who's lately become a household face, thanks to the frequent, impromptu televised press briefings which you seem to be forever setting up for yourself?

BROWNIE. Press briefings are all part of the job, sir.

PROCTOR. Press briefings sometimes are the job, wouldn't you say?

BROWNIE. No respect intended, Senator, but I think that first and uppermost the American people need to be informed of all actions undertaken by their federal government at every single time in time.

PROCTOR. And in my belief, the general impression you've given, in my opinion, is that despite repeated warnings, warnings that persisted right up until the eve of the disaster, the complete cluelessness at COMA's, combined with your absolutely utter enuptitude helped to create what was to become a virtual tsunami of imbecility.

ALEXANDER. Mister Chairman!

GROSS. *(overlapping)* Mister Brownie?

BROWNIE. Sir?

GROSS. Would you care to respond to the senator's question-slash vicious attack?

BROWNIE. I would be most grateful, sir, if you could allow me a short moment of opportunistism.

GROSS. You may do whatever you like with your microphone.

BROWNIE. Thank you, sir. Yes, we might indeed have been warned as you say we were, Senator Proctor, but positively no one could ever have predicted that the events that wound up happening were events that would actually ever of happened at all. And that, sir, is something that has been agreed upon by nearly everyone in this administration from the president on up!

GROSS. Thank you, Mister Brownie.

BROWNIE. Thank you, Mister Chairman.

GROSS. I take it you are finished with the witness, Senator Proctor?

PROCTOR. As far as I'm concerned he is.

ALEXANDER. Mister Chairman!

GROSS. The Chair recognizes Congresswoman Alexander.

ALEXANDER. Forgive me, Mister Chairman, but I am finding it increasingly difficult having my silence go unheard here.

THE VOICE OVER. Floodgate marked junior representative Virginia Alexander's first committee appearance since winning custody of her late husband's Congressional seat as part of their divorce settlement - Her husband's private plane crashing and burning six months after their marriage did exactly the same thing.

ALEXANDER. I find the baiting of the witness by my distinguished colleague to be the worst kind of badgering that I have ever seen.

PROCTOR. In all of your one whole week in Congress, madam?

ALEXANDER. Congress it may to you, sir. To me, it is the very liberty house that freedom itself built. Built on the blood spilled by those brave young men and women whose choice it was never to cut and run in the face of overwhelming logic.

PROCTOR. Mister Chairman, may I suggest the good lady rise to her feet and consider standing, in order to avoid the danger of wrinkling her flag?

(murmering from **THE COMMITTEE***)*

(sound: gavel, gavel, gavel)

THE VOICE OVER. At the conclusion of the shambles, attorney Lowell Dickler addressed the committee in yet or more attempt to justify his exorbitant fee.

DICKLER. Mister Chairman? I wonder, sir, if the committee has no further questions of him whether the witness might be allowed to use the opening statement that he never got make and deliver it as his closing statement instead?

GROSS. In the interests of redundancy, the Chair will re-recognize the witness.

BROWNIE. Thank you, Senator. Although there has been a great deal of finger pointing yo, these many months, I think the time has come when I can no longer go on taking all of the credit for my miserable performance. I must say that had the local authorities acted in a more professional manner - had the members of the D.C. police and fire departments of the opposite political and color persuasion filled out the proper forms and applications which COMA requires of even those people who know what they are doing – Had they learned to act by the play book instead of racing around town willynilly, hoping to rescue a few dying hospital patients here, or trying to put out the odd house on fire there –In short, had they not, in general, tried coping with all of the turmoil they saw all around them on an ad hoc, person-byperson, victim-by-victim basis – Had they given the bureaucracy a fair chance to

BROWNIE. *(cont.)* prove itself, I know for a fact that it would have been no trouble at all for us to cut the chaos in half in only twice the time. In closing, I can't say enough about how grateful I am for the many, many wonderful subpoenas that I've received from this and numerous other congressional committees, each of which will allow me the chance of expressing myself to the extent that only a born scapegoat can truly appreciate. I thank the committee for allowing me this moment of selfindulgence. But that is something that no one else can really do for you. My thanks to the Chair, as well. Chateau to you, sir.

GROSS. Thank you, Mister Brownie. Let me assure you that the committee will express its proper gratitude once we obtain and fill out the correct forms required for that purpose.

BROWNIE. And you'll have my response just as soon as I can, sir.

GROSS. You are excused.

BROWNIE. I can only hope so. Thank you, sir.

(*sound: gavel*)

THE VOICE OVER. For its next witness, the committee called upon the frequently put-upon Secretary of the Office for the Security of the Homeland against International Terror and Extremists.

GROSS. The Secretary will please state his name for the record.

CHERKOFF. I am Michael Cherkoff, Mister Chairman.

GROSS. Please stand, Mister Cherkoff.

THE VOICE OVER. One of the most prestigious Cherkoffs in Washington, D.C., Michael Cherkoff is a direct descendant of Jeremiah Cherkoff, chief political advisor to Aaron Burr.

GROSS. Raise your right hand, if you would.

CHERKOFF. It is so raised, sir.

THE VOICE OVER. After swearing in the witness, the Cherkoff testimony began.

CHERKOFF. *(finishing)* So help me God.

GROSS. Please be seated.

CHERKOFF. Thank you, sir.

GROSS. If the Secretary will please state his official title for the record?

CHERKOFF. I am the head, Mister Chairman, of the Office for the Security of the Homeland against International Terror and Extremists.

GROSS. OSHITE.

CHERKOFF. OSHITE. Yes, sir.

GROSS. Congresswoman Alexander? You have ten minutes - and not one hour more.

ALEXANDER. Thank you, Mister Chairman. Good morning, Mister Secretary.

CHERKOFF. Congressma'am.

ALEXANDER. Allow me a moment of my time, if you would, sir, for me to fawn, if I may, over what I consider your magnificent handling of the calamitous events that befell upon our capital, plus the ensuement of the confusion and anarchy which followed, regardless of the almost wall-to-wall carping to which you were then and to which you still continuously seem to find your-self on the receiving end of.

CHERKOFF. It's easy enough I guess for some folks to forget that the scale of the assault on Washington, D.C. was far and beyond any previous precedent.

ALEXANDER. The tipping point being in your opinion, what, sir?

CHERKOFF. If I had to put it in one word, that word would be march.

ALEXANDER. March of this year?

CHERKOFF. Not March, the month. The million family one that took place against the government claiming it had illegally tapped their combined seven and a half million phones. As you know, their number soon swelled by a hundred, then finally, easily a thousand morefold. The streets became clogged with so many protesters, posters and placards, eventually there was nowhere near enough room for so many families to find a place in which to fall down in after being gassed by either the police, the army, or any of the freelance personnel that were assigned to make the people feel secure. There was hardly even enough room for the hundreds of young children who were overcome, even as they sang that very same song. Worst of possibly all to me was the media's saturation of the public with its ceaseless, liberal doses of footage that repeatedly emphasized scenes of negativity, creating an image which only served to misconstrue the public over and over again.

ALEXANDER. That is a sad talking point indeed, sir.

CHERKOFF. Yes, ma'am.

ALEXANDER. On the media in general, Mister Secretary, I'd be interested in knowing just how much you agree with me about something.

CHERKOFF. Offhand, I'd say a hundred percent'd probably be about half right.

ALEXANDER. I'm referring to the press' obsession with the need to always paint the darkest possible picture. Especially about our brightest achievements.

CHERKOFF. Criticism is the sour mother's milk of journalism, ma'am. No offense.

ALEXANDER. Tell us about the looting spree that refutedly took place in the capital, if you would, Mister Secretary, after the city was swamped on Eleven-Nine. Would you say that that situation was as bad as it was as the medias made it out to be? As immediate?

CHERKOFF. Regrettably, that is one of the truer facts that was misreported. A good deal of historical material, was indeed carried off by the first absconders. Starting with what I'm afraid was an unauthorized change of the original Gettysburg Address.

ALEXANDER. Lincoln's speech was stolen?

CHERKOFF. By some of the people, yes, ma'am.

ALEXANDER. Any other thefts come to mind?

CHERKOFF. There were so many, really, it's hard —There was a first draft of the Bill of Rights, I remember that. With some of the coffee cup rings still visible on it. Then there was the looting of several major pieces of antiquity – irreplaceable pieces that had been recovered from the looting of the Baghdad Museum and brought to America for safe keeping.

ALEXANDER. There were reports that the U.S. Mint and Treasury were both hit hard.

CHERKOFF. What really happened was the sort of success story that the press is always so reluctant to report. Thanks to this president's economic policies, there was absolutely no money at all left to be stolen. All the looters managed to get away with was roughly eight trillion dollars in IOUs held by the People's First Bank of Beijing.

THE VOICE OVER. Following a break which allowed the members of the committee to vote an additional twenty-two billion dollars in immediate relief aid to themselves, the Cherkoff questioning was taken up again by the deputy acting committee assistant minority leader, Senator Lester Stillbourne.

STILLBOURNE. Good day, Mister Secretary.

CHERKOFF. I'll take all of those I can get, Senator.

STILLBOURNE. Please rest assured I'm not going to keep you any longer than I'm allowed to, appreciating as I do the danger we all face every minute that you're in charge of our security.

CHERKOFF. Thank you, sir. Everyone who knows me shares that concern.

STILLBOURNE. Speaking at an earlier moment in time, you referenced your experience as a judge, would I be right in remembering that correctly?

CHERKOFF. For the purpose of answering that particular question, I would have to say that you are.

STILLBOURNE. I can take that as a yes?

CHERKOFF. I believe my response can be seen to fit that paradigm.

STILLBOURNE. Would you please inform the committee just when and where it was that you last served in any sort of jurisprudical capacity?

CHERKOFF. The last time I acted as a judge?

STILLBOURNE. If that's what I said, yes.

CHERKOFF. That would have been in 1998, sir.

STILLBOURNE. And where in that particular year in time would that have been?

CHERKOFF. In Nogano, Japan, sir.

STILLBOURNE. Nogano, Japan. Would that have been at the – ?

CHERKOFF. At the Winter Olympics, yes, sir.

STILLBOURNE. At the Winter Olympics in Nogano, Japan?

CHERKOFF. Hi!

STILLBOURNE. That is Japanese for "yes," is it not?

CHERKOFF. Hi.

STILLBOURNE. And anything after that that you might care to tell us about?

CHERKOFF. Quite a bit more, Senator, if you factor in the number of years I served as a consultant, first, at ESPN, and then later, for ABC's "*Wide World of Sports.*"

STILLBOURNE. Again serving as a consultant?

CHERKOFF. Yes, sir. Although I did, from time to time, continue acting as a judge at the occasional charity ice show.

STILLBOURNE. Judging ice skaters then was your real specialty.

CHERKOFF. Once I gave up skating myself, yes, sir.

STILLBOURNE. You were also a professional skater?

CHERKOFF. Ice is in my blood, sir.

STILLBOURNE. Given that that is a requirement for serving in this particular administration, did it ever once strike you that, given your background, becoming this country's chief of security was just a tiniest bit of a stretch?

CHERKOFF. Not really, Senator. Both jobs call for cool headed thinking under pressure; both require setting a certain standard of performance.

STILLBOURNE. And what kind of a score would you say you would give yourself, using your own Cherkoff standard, when it comes to your performance in the recent D.C. debacle?

CHERKOFF. Any particular aspect of it, sir?

STILLBOURNE. Those aspects of it for which you have been so almost uniformly and roundly condemned.

CHERKOFF. A bit of specificity would be very helpful, sir. I've been condemned for so much and by so many lately, I'd say I've gotten an almost perfect ten in condemnation.

STILLBOURNE. Let's start with your wretched, inexcusably reprehensible handling of the refugees from the Senate and House of Representatives, shall we? Can you tell us whose idea was it, for instance, for all of the legislators and their families to be rounded up and crowded into RFK stadium?

CHERKOFF. That order was one that came straight from the top, sir.

STILLBOURNE. From the president?

CHERKOFF. I said the top, sir.

STILLBOURNE. You had to go one step down to go one step up?

CHERKOFF. To the best of my ability to try avoiding any blame, I would have to say it was the vice president's plan - the plan that we use RFK stadium as a holding area.

STILLBOURNE. A holding area for government officials.

CHERKOFF. Until we could get them to higher, safer ground, yes, sir, somewhere away from the usual low road.

STILLBOURNE. And all of the confusion and pandemonium that followed – all of that was part of the same plan?

CHERKOFF. You can't plan on confusion, sir. It's only after it breaks out that you realize you're dealing with something you can't deal with. If you're referring to the turmoil that followed amongst the senators and the congressmen once they found themselves locked inside the stadium - all of the fighting and the violence that broke out: Mainly, what I believe, sir? I believe it was largely a matter of them all wanting to have seats on the 50 yard line.

STILLBOURNE. But it was you, was it not, who issued the order that they all be moved to the Carter Barron Amphitheater?

CHERKOFF. I was much more familiar with the Amphitheater, Senator, having once given Michelle Kwan a perfect set of marks in that same building in spite of both of us having a pulled groin.

STILLBOURNE. Better marks than the ones I'm afraid I would give you, sir, considering the number of reported instances there have been of all of the mob rape and abuse that was heaped upon so many of the members of our members.

CHERKOFF. I can only think that there were those among the mob who wanted to do to our legislators what they felt our legislators have been doing to them for years, sir. In any case, I did what I thought was best at the time, Senator. Nobody skates with a rear-view mirror, y'know. The truth to one side? Of all the charges that I've been privy to - charges ranging from cronyism to charges of incompetency, to charges of incompetent cronyism - There's not a single one of them that rankles me harder than the charge that I was quicker to evacuate white members of the Congress than I was those of its black members who tended to be American-Africans. If there is one thing I have proudly worn as a badge of honor over the years, it is the manner in which I have always stood upon any person of any color whatsoever.

GROSS. Thank you, Mister Secretary.

CHERKOFF. Thank you, Mister Senator.

(sound: gavel)

THE VOICE OVER. Before returning to highlights of the Floodgate hearings, here a few AGN program notes - a reminder of our other coverage of the current of events as depicted in a rash of new literature. At noon, Eastern Standard Time, the celebrated and discredited author, Arthur Kribbman, will discuss his number one best seller, "Embed with the Enemy," a true account of how a celebrated newspaper journalist falsified report after report during the fighting in Gulf One. Mister Kribbman, who based his accounts on earlier accounts of earlier wars by earlier celebrated newspaper journalists, is the recipient of the two thousand and five prestigious National Plagiarist Award for the best fictional writing of a non-fiction book. Then, at one, Washington Diary will play host to the former Tree Surgeon General of the United States, Dr. Philip J. Landfill. Dr. Landfill, recently resigned from the think tank which he helped found, The Allied Movement to Protect American Conservatism, is leaving his desk at TAMPAC to serve as head of the newlyformed bureau of Federal Emergency Housing, or FEH. Dr. Landfill will discuss his controversial book, "Learn to Clone," alternating the reading of various passages with six of his eight brothers. At two o'clock, Eastern Standard Time, William Carbon will talk about his best selling "Twin Embeds," Carbon's account of a fellow journalist's fraudulent reporting of military actions in the fighting that occurred during Gulf Two. Mister Carbon will take your questions about the charges of plagiarism that have been leveled against him by last week's guest author, Mister Arthur Kribbman. Following that, Mister Kribbman will discuss one of his many forthcoming law suits which allege that whole chapters of William Carbon's book were stolen wholesale from certain of Mister Kribbman's stolen chapters. Here now, are further excerpts from the Floodgate hearings.

GROSS. Before introducing our next panel of witnesses, the Chair would like to share the following letter which I am just in receipt of from the President of the United States.

(reads)

"Firstly, let me express my thanks to the committee for accepting the terms of my willingness to be cooperative as I can be provided I can appear in the company of my vice president. "A man who, like me, is one hundred percent committed, as a great many people have long felt that he ought to be. "Having him at my side will allow me to testify to the best of both of our abilities. "In any event, two heads are always better than none. "Being a president who means to stand behind everything I say he does, and believing that I can best assist your select panel with the help of those whose memories are even more selective than my own, I am planning on also being accompanied by a second member of my personal staff: my chief of Strategic Spinning. "With every expectation that I can count on the Chairman's reputation for abjectivity, I assure you that both my vice president and my top SS man are all looking forward to my joint appearance before you. "Dedicated as we are, not for playing the game blame but for finding out who is really responsible for so many of the things that I have taken responsibility for, I remain, for as long as it is humanly possible, the President of this God blessed America."

(Once again, the president's words cause an audible stir among **THE COMMITTEE.***)*

STILLBOURNE. Mister Chairman!

(a gavel, then:)

GROSS. Order. Order.

STILLBOURNE. Just what is the President of the United States afraid of, Mister Chairman?

GROSS. Order!

STILLBOURNE. Why this need for a Pretolian Guard to protect him against the dangers of the truth, the whole truth, so he can tell us anything but the truth?

GROSS. This is not a president who is shirkful of any dangers, Senator.

STILLBOURNE. Or one who is any way shy when it comes to misusing his arrogance.

PROCTOR. You give him an inch, he takes a foot.

STILLBOURNE. You give him a foot, he makes it a prosthesis. Murmur, murmur.

(sound: gavel)

ALEXANDER. Good lord, are we going to start flinging body parts at one another?

(sound: gavel)

GROSS. If it would calm the minority, the Chair will entertain a vote on the president's latest request, a request, which to my eye I might add, is as sincere and innocent as the blue crayola with which it was signed.

PROCTOR. Perhaps the Chair might explain the necessity for taking a vote, the sum total of which we all know is already quite snugly in the bag.

GROSS. Be that as it may, and I have no doubt that it will, after the next round of questions, I suggest we take the matter up in camera, away from the already far too many we have all around us as it is.

(Sound: Gavel. Gavel.)

GROSS. Now, if we might just have the names of our next witnesses, please, however household they may be? First, you, sir?

WITNESS. My name is Ronald Dumsfeld.

GROSS. Can you tell us please the position which you held, sir, in the administration at the question in time into which this committee is looking?

DUMSFELD. I was, at that particular then in time, Mister Chairman serving in the cabinet as the President's SOD.

GROSS. His Sod.

DUMSFELD. His Secretary of Defense, sir.

GROSS. And if your fellow, just as distinguished, witness could also so identify himself, please?

NYER. I am multi-starred and hugely decorated General Richard D. Nyer, Mister Chairman.

GROSS. You are, of course, sir, the Chief of the Joint Chiefs of Staff.

NYER. Actually, I'm its Chairman, Mister Chairman.

GROSS. Knowing how busy both of you gentlemen are, the members of the committee deeply appreciate you taking the time out so that we may appear before you here today. Is there anything you'd like to say, Mister Secretary, before you say anything at all, sir?

DUMSFELD. I've prepared nothing special, Mister Chairman. I'm a great believer in going with my own flow. Why don't we just start in and we can both find out what it is I'm saying at the same time?

GROSS. I thought perhaps you might want to use this forum to address the many number of critics who have given you so much heat within the tenure of your present time frame.

DUMSFELD. If it quacks like a duck, those people just roll off my back, Mister Chairman. In my book, patriotism trumps criticism every time. Just as extremism in the defense of liberty is no vice, moderation in the pursuit of justice is no virtue.

GROSS. Well put.

DUMSFELD. I made that up.

GROSS. Wasn't it Barry Goldwater who said it first?

DUMSFELD. It's not uncommon for two people to come up with the same idea, y'know.

GROSS. True enough.

DUMSFELD. We need only look at the Wright Brothers.

GROSS. If you will not, Mister Secretary, then I would like to take a moment of personal privilege to say how deeply

I appreciate all that you have managed to do to this country in such a relatively short period. Even in perilest of these darktimes, your efforts have provided the nation with the certainty of knowing just how much darker they could still become. For that, these particular United States in time will never forget you, sir.

DUMSFELD. Nor I them, Mister Chairman.

GROSS. General Nyer.

NYER. Sir?

GROSS. How do you rebutt, sir, to those who charge that our military was unable to be all that it could be in coming to the aid of our former capital during the period of its recent, historic befallment? And, as a follow-up monologue, would you share with us what lessons you might have drawn from this experience that could ever possibly be of any use to anyone else at all?

NYER. Let me prioritize my response by first assuring the American people that every man, woman and child in our armed forces performed their duties with the same courage and obviousness that I see reflected back at me in the grateful and gratuitous displays of support stickers brandished everywhere on the nation's SUVs, for whose mileage so many of them were so proud to have given their lives for.

DUMSFELD. If I may interject the general?

GROSS. Without objection, I'm sure.

DUMSFELD. Only to say to those who say that the only purpose of our military mission in the Middle East is to control the flow of terrorist oil, our studies show that by configuring our casualties with the ever escalating cost of the overruns incurred in the process of overrunning the enemy overseas instead of over our backyard fence, that we are still managing on getting an almost unprecedented average of two and half lives to the gallon.

GROSS. Thank you, Mister Secretary.

DUMSFELD. I'll just let the general finish whatever else it is I have to say.

NYER. Thank you, sir. In the lessons learned department, Senator?

GROSS. If you please.

NYER. I would have to say it's having the sure knowledge that no amount of advance planning can ever prepare anyone for what an unexpected leadership is going to ask of you.

GROSS. Well put, sir.

NYER. As you were.

GROSS. Senator Proctor?

PROCTOR. Mister Secretary.

DUMSFELD. Senator Proctor.

PROCTOR. General Nyer.

DUMSFELD. Senator Proctor.

PROCTOR. This is a question for either one of you.

NYER. Yes, sir.

PROCTOR. The events of Eleven-Nine - they took place on Eleven-Nine, is that correct?

DUMSFELD. According to my records, those two dates occurred on the very same day, yes, sir.

NYER. I copy.

PROCTOR. an either of you explain then, in light of the diresome events that took place on that particular time in date, how it happened that it wasn't until ten whole days later, on Eleven-Nineteen, when the Defense Department finally chose to act in any manner whatsoever at all?

DUMSFELD. If we so-called "failed" to act, Senator –

PROCTOR. The Secretary will excuse me, but I didn't use the word "if," sir. What I said was "when."

DUMSFELD. Well, what is an "if" if it's not a "when" that is just waiting for its time to become one? An ifness, per see, does not, in any case, cancel out the possibility of a whenness. Or do you see it another way, sir?

PROCTOR. I'm not sure I even know what it is we're discussing anymore.

DUMSFELD. I'm a great believer in talking without a net, Senator. If I can be entrusted to intuit the thrust of your insinuation, it seems quite obviously an inferral that my folks were tardy incoming to the aid of those who were imperiled by the events that had overtaken the capital. To which I can only opinionate that by not acting in any way at all, I was acting completely in compliance with the law.

PROCTOR. There is a law against springing into action? One that keeps you from being helpful?

DUMSFELD. There are many such laws on the books, Senator. I'm referring to the one that's not coy about it.

PROCTOR. That law being what, sir?

DUMSFELD. The PCA, sir.

PROCTOR. And for those with no knowledge of the PCA?

DUMSFELD. The PCA is the Posse Cacamaimus Act.

PROCTOR. Posse Cacamaimus? Could you be more elaborate?

DUMSFELD. General?

NYER. What the Secretary is referencing to, Senator, is Title 10 of the United States Code, Directive 55235, such directive clearly stating that the PCA precludes, prevents, and prohibits the armed forces from direct participation in any civic search, seizure, and/or arrest.

PROCTOR. Surely, the expertise of our armed forces could have been helpful in other capacities? Something other than making arrests or causing seizures? Say, aiding or assisting refugees perhaps? Maybe transporting casualties?

DUMSFELD. I'm not unaware of the Senator's repeated innurendoes that our armed forces were too otherwise engaged abroad, creating new refugees and causing new casualties altogether elsewhere in the world.

PROCTOR. If the boot fits, Mister Secretary.

DUMSFELD. Let me assure you, sir, that the presence of our military in a multiplicity of other ZOOCS had at the very worst a minimal to nil impact as to how we treated the upheavement that was brewing back in Washington.

PROCTOR. ZOOCS?

NYER. Zones of Other Conflict.

DUMSFELD. Places not lucky enough to be America, or even a tenth as free as we used to be. Zones where our unstinting troops maintain a relentless mission of liberation and the imposition of freedom, unmindful of the dangers they risk by constantly exposing themselves to everyone they meet.

PROCTOR. Such situations being exactly where at this particular now in time? A check list perhaps of where we are presently – at the present?

DUMSFELD. Well, for openers, there is, of course, Iraq, of course.

PROCTOR. An oldie, but a goody.

DUMSFELD. The general's probably a whole lot more up on all this than I am. Running half a dozen war's hard enough without have to know which one of 'em's where.

NYER. Let me take it alphabetically for you, Senator: You've got your Afghanistan. Your Bosnia. Iran. Lebanon. North Korea. Palestine. Syria.

DUMSFELD. Taiwan, with a bullet.

PROCTOR. You don't think, Mister Secretary, that, under your guidance, our forces are not being stretched just a little too thin?

DUMSFELD. You can never be too free or too thin, Senator.

PROCTOR. If not our personnel, then, what about the charge that we could not use our best equipment in our most recent emergency because so much of it had been deployed overseas to decimate however many people we can in the interest of spreading democracy?

DUMSFELD. That charge is as groundless as a cup of army coffee, sir.

PROCTOR. Our best equipment is not overseas?

NYER. Just ask our troops, Senator.

PROCTOR. Just where would you say our very best equipment is then, General?

NYER. The truth department? The truth is that at this particular time in point, this country has zero to no best equipment at all.

PROCTOR. None?

DUMSFELD. Possibly less.

PROCTOR. That is a stunning statement, Mister Secretary.

DUMSFELD. Thank you.

PROCTOR. What in your best hindsight would be the reason that – ?

(sound: gavel)

PROCTOR. I can't believe the Chair is cutting me off in mid–

GROSS. I'm afraid the senator doesn't realize he's expired. Senator Stillbourne? I assume you have a few queries you would like to pose?

STILLBOURNE. Thank you, Mister Chairman. Mister Secretary, you continue to quarrel with the premise, do you, sir, that, despite the fact that 99 out of the hundred thousand retired generals on TV insist that such is the case, that the dispersal of so much of our troopage in no way imperils our possible need for military assistance in any un-or-even-forseen home front disaster?

DUMSFELD. Putting our warheads together at the Pentagon, I believe we've devised a rather elegant solution, one which, is simplexity itself.

STILLBOURNE. We, for one, would be most anxious to learn such a plan might be, sir.

DUMSFELD. I can appreciate that, Senator, but I'm afraid the details are of such a highly classified nature, none of us is as yet allowed to completely understand what it is that we've come up with. Does the general wish to subtract anything from what I've just said?

NYER. I would only add that it will soon be available to the members of Congress in the form of a white paper that's been titled the "Reallocation of Base and Barracks Initiative."

STILLBOURNE. The Reallocation of Base –

DUMSFELD. *(cuts in)* RABBI.

STILLBOURNE. Got it.

DUMSFELD. RABBI, is a series of variable scenarios based on probable homegrown rather than exported disasters. What it proposes is the creation of one central National Guard unit, whose responsibility it would be to service the needs of every state in the union.

NYER. It works out to about one guardsman or guardswoman for every quarter of a million people.

STILLBOURNE. Does that seem enough to you, General? Considering the everincreasing number of floods, earthquakes, typhoons, hurricanes, tornadoes, and other possible effects of the ruinous global warming this administration assures us can never occur due to the flatness of planet?

DUMSFELD. I can promise you there'll be more than enough relief support - once there are fewer people for every guardsman.

NYER. We're working out the metrics.

DUMSFELD. *(overlapping)* We've worked out the metrics.

STILLBOURNE. Wouldn't it simpler to bring home some of our troops from some of the theaters of war in which they are currently performing?

DUMSFELD. You send a mixed bag of signals, Senator, bringing troops home before their missions have been declared accomplished, especially the ones that haven't got a chance in hell of ever being so. Trust me, we're not going to be short of any manpower. One aspect of RABBI calls for increasing the size of our armed forces through the more vigorous recruitment of the homeless, the incarcerated and the pre-deranged. I do hope the Chair is watching the clock?

THE VOICE OVER. Secretary Dumsfeld understandingly anxious about the time, was also scheduled to appear before the Senate Judiciary and Vigorish Committee for confirmation hearings in connection with his recent appointment as Associate Justice to the Supreme Court. Although approval came swiftly, the Secretary could not take his seat on the bench until the successful appeal of his own indictment as a war criminal at the International Court trials on charges of violating Articles One through Ninety-Seven of the Geneva Conventions, relating to recreational torture and the acceptable length of dogleashes. As well as his also having violated both the Sixth and Ninth Commandments: "Thousand shalt not kill" and "Thou shalt not bear false witness."

GROSS. The committee thanks you, General, for your always dazzling appearance of confidence.

NYER. Thank you, Mister Chairman.

GROSS. And our thanks to you, Mister Secretary. Or are you more comfortable with "Justice?"

DUMSFELD. That'll take some getting used to. Thank you, Senator. Thank you all. Except the press, of course.

(gavel)

VOICE OVER. The committee then declared a two week hiatus, during which the members of both houses of Congress were flown by private plane, and then comped to the Wounded Knee Golf Tournament, which were held at the Massacre Hilton in Pierre, South Dakota. On the committee's first morning back, the resumed hearings began with a bombshell.

STILLBOURNE. Mister Chairman?

GROSS. Senator Stillbourne, you wish to be recognized?

STILLBOURNE. I would gladly sacrifice recognition for information, Mister Chairman.

GROSS. The sort of which is what?

STILLBOURNE. I would gladly sacrifice recognition for information, Mister Chairman. My staff has just learned from all ninwty-seven cable news channels something I would have thought members of this committee would certainly have learned first from you, Mister Chairman.

GROSS. And may I know just what it is my learned friend has learned?

STILLBOURNE. That, according to accredited, impeccable leakers, this committee is in receipt of yet another communication from the temporary White House. One with yet one more presidential condition regarding the appearance that the president has pledged to make before us.

(Murmurs. Gavel.)

GROSS. All my cable stations having shut down for yet another unauthorized price hike, I have not as yet seen any TV today. Therefore, I can't say for a fact that anything, officially, has actually happened at all. This would not be the first time that newsmakers have to watch the news to find out just what sort of news it is that we have made.

STILLBOURNE. With the Chair's permission, I will read a transcript of the president's new demands regarding his testification before this committee.

GROSS. Without objection.

STILLBOURNE. That's what you think.

GROSS. Just read.

STILLBOURNE. *(reads)* "To the Chairman of the Oversight Committee from the undersigned President of the United States, for which I so proudly stand. "Let me first express my thanks for the promptness of the committee's capitulation. "Both the vice president and similarly my chief advisor share my eagerness to present our version of what it is that I am being prepared to think about regarding the role that I played that might possibly have worsened the goings on of whatever it was that went on, a condition, I am told, that has been known to afflict as many as ten out of nine presidents. "Any misgivings of appearing live before a sitting committee notwithstanding, there remains only the matter of scheduling such an appearance that I have been told I am only too pleased to make. "Such scheduling is made somewhat difficult at the time of this moment, since my schedule calls upon me to make three trips to Europe next week, following which I am going to have to leave the country."

PROCTOR. You're making this up.

STILLBOURNE. Would that I were.

GROSS. Read on.

STILLBOURNE. *(reads)*"Should the Chair find the date as suitable as it does me, we can safely pencil in fifteen minutes on the fifteenth of this month for me to give you my official recollection of the events into which you are seeking. "Acting upon the advice of my counselor, as well as the counsel of my advisor, I therefore request a single member of your committee's choosing, accompanied by a small camera crew of one, to report to the temporary White House on the above said date in time for the purpose of taping whatever helpful testimony your representative may be able to drudge forth from me "Trusting your response will meet my every expectation, I somehow still manage to remain the president of the eckcetera, eckcetera." That's it, Mister Chairman.

GROSS. Thank you, Mister Stillbourne.

PROCTOR. Mister Chairman!

GROSS. There being no objection, I will have staff look into the feasabilityness of the date so designated in the aforeread.

PROCTOR. Mister Chairman! Mister Chairman!

GROSS. For what purpose does the gentleman's ire rise? And in triplicate, no less?

PROCTOR. Mister Chairman, sir! Firstly, we are informed by the President of the United States of America that he cannot appear before this committee unless he is accompanied by the vice president of these same United States of this very same America.

GROSS. Unless you have something new to add, sir, that is very old indeed, sir.

PROCTOR. Then, we are informed that the Chief Advisor to the Chief Executive is also to be present during the question and answer period, presumably to comfort the president by holding his hand just in case there happen to be any scary parts. And then, now, this! This demand, all dressed up as a stipulation, that the presidential appearance we have been promised is to be taped. That having deigned to appear before us, the President of the United States will not be appearing before us at all. That all he is offering the committee is the appearance of an appearance - an appearance that merely gives the appearance that one has been made at all.

GROSS. And what, pray tell, if you are able to tell us, is the difference between an actual appearance and one that only appears to be one?

PROCTOR. I don't pretend to be an expert, Mister Chairman, but I think I know an appearance when I see one.

GROSS. And that is exactly what the President of the United States is willing to make, as he has taken such pains to inform us, starting with and through the press.

STILLBOURNE. Mister Chairman?

GROSS. Senator Stillbourne?

STILLBOURNE. Can you tell me why on earth, sir, the president should be allowed to dictate the amount of time that this committee would want to put him through, whether he's on tape or whether he's alive? Fifteen minutes, that's all he's willing to spare us? Fifteen minutes?!

GROSS. Can anyone deny that this is a president whose time is very valuable?

STILLBOURNE. To be as pithy as I can, I am one of those people who deny that he is even a president at all.

(Murmur, murmur.)

GROSS. The Chair has no intention whatsoever of getting into a pithy contest with my distinguished colleague.

(sound: gavel)

THE VOICE OVER. And so the stage was set for the President of the United States to make his taped appearance, one that was later to be played before the committee and, by extension, to the very United States of which he was the president of. On the afternoon of the fifteenth of the following month in time, facing a lone camera in the Broken Treaty Room of the temporary White House, a confident president appeared in the company of his vice president and chief presidential advisor, Karl Strangerove.

MALE VOICE. Good morning, Mister President.

THE VOICE OVER. First to address the Chief Executive was the committee's counsel - former prosecutor, retired judge, and occasional defendant himself, Mister Simian Pandergast.

PANDERGAST. I am Chief Counsel for the Oversight Committee, Mister President.

THE VOICE OVER. Quick to respond were the vice president–

THE VICE PRESIDENT. We know who you are, Mister Pandergast.

THE VOICE OVER. – And the president's chief advisor.

THE CHIEF ADVISOR. We know where you live, too.

PANDERGAST. Good morning, gentlemen.

THE VICE PRESIDENT. We'll see.

PANDERGAST. If I might ask the president to please place your hand on the bible, sir?

THE PRESIDENT. You kiddin' me? I walk around with my hand on it all day long.

PANDERGAST. That's easy enough to believe, sir, but I need for you to take the oath, Mister President.

THE PRESIDENT. Again? I haven't touched a drop in years. Jes' funnin' ya. Y'wanna slug'a this water? It's refreshin'.

PANDERGAST. Thank you, no. I'm fine, sir.

THE PRESIDENT. Go ahead, then. Do yer stuff.

(takes a sip, then)

Shoot.

(aside) Stop blushin', Dick. Y'wanna watch yourself, Mister Pandyman. Y'don' wanna be comin' up behind the ole Dickster here.

PANDERGAST. Yes, sir. Now, then, do you swear, Mister President, that the testimony I hope you are about to give will be the truth, the whole truth, and nothing but the truth, so help you God?

THE VICE PRESIDENT. He does.

PANDERGAST. I'm sorry, Mister Vice President, but the president has to answer that himself.

THE PRESIDENT. You heard him, Pandster. Consider me sworn.

PANDERGAST. But, sir, you haven't actually in fact –

THE PRESIDENT. Consider me in the same class as the Attorney General, in that we're both immune from the truth, y'know what I – ?

PANDERGAST. *(overlapping)* Well, that, too, was a bit –

THE PRESIDENT. Let me finish here, okay?

THE CHIEF ADVISOR. Let him finish.

THE VICE PRESIDENT. He may have had a thought.

THE PRESIDENT. I don' remember what it was now. It's gone. Ya made me miss the whole train.

PANDERGAST. I'm sorry, Mister President.

THE PRESIDENT. I hate finishin' before I'm not, y'know what I mean? I'm not a big fan'a idea interruptus. What y'wanna do is sit aroun' here in my shoes fer jes' one day, okay? You'd learn soon enough the nessarity fer delegatin' authority.

PANDERGAST. I'm sure that must be true, sir.

THE PRESIDENT. Ya don' think it's hard work, bein' head cheese-in-chief of a whole country? It's a whole lot harder'n anyone knows. Take my word, there's no president worth his salt that's perverse ta gettin' all the help he can. Y'know what else stops where you 'n I are sittin', shootin' the breeze right now? Beside the buck? The truth stops here. Take it from me.

THE CHIEF ADVISOR. If the vice president swears the president's going to be nothing but truthful –

THE PRESIDENT. His word ought'a be good enough for the both of us.

PANDERGAST. I was only doing my –

THE PRESIDENT. Y'jes' gonna ask a whole lotta questions without waitin' fer an answer, is zat your game plan, Pandarama?

PANDERGAST. No, sir.

THE VICE PRESIDENT. I believe you were fully briefed on the ground rules by the White House Counselor, Counselor?

PANDERGAST. I was briefed at length, yes, sir.

THE CHIEF ADVISOR. Then just remember Rule One: never interrupt the president when he's talking. He hates that.

THE VICE PRESIDENT. When he talks, you don't.

THE CHIEF ADVISOR. Given our new time constraints, I suggest you assign one of your eyes to the clock, Mister Pandergast.

THE VICE PRESIDENT. You've already wasted –

PANDERGAST. *(cuts in)* New time constraints? I wasn't told that there'd been any change in the –

THE CHIEF ADVISOR. *(cuts in)* You're not to interrupt the vice president either.

PANDERGAST. I'm sorry, sir. I knew my time was circumscribed. I didn't know it had been further cut off.

THE CHIEF ADVISOR. A reason is not an excuse around here, Counselor.

PANDERGAST. I appreciate that, sir –

THE CHIEF ADVISOR. There's room for just so much ignorance at this level of government.

PANDERGAST. Yes, sir.

THE VICE PRESIDENT. The fact is the president's due for a sudden photo op in the Rose Garden in ten minutes from this particular now.

PANDERGAST. In ten – ?

THE CHIEF ADVISOR. He's set to pose with the Illegal Immigrant of the Year.

THE VICE PRESIDENT. Who, as it turns out, is the same man who looks after the Rose Garden.

THE PRESIDENT. Who'd'a thunk it, huh? Man, that Javier's got some pair'a huevos.

PANDERGAST. Just so I know where I am: has the clock started for me yet, Mister Vice President?

THE VICE PRESIDENT. From the minute you left your office.

THE CHIEF ADVISOR. Are you ready then, Mister President?

THE PRESIDENT. All suited up. Let's roll, Pandemic.

PANDERGAST. I thought we might start by creating a timeline of the first day of the events of Eleven-Nine, Mister President. A reconstruction of the events, if we might, if you would?

THE PRESIDENT. Reconstruction's good. Let's ya start buildin' all over again.

PANDERGAST. If you could tell the committee just exactly where you were when you heard the first reports of the flooding that were starting to pour in.

THE PRESIDENT. Gotcha.

PANDERGAST. *(After a pause)* Sir?

THE PRESIDENT. I'm thinkin'.

THE VICE PRESIDENT. Let him finish.

THE PRESIDENT. Can't jes' jump start that process, y'know.

PANDERGAST. Of course.

THE PRESIDENT. Dickmeister, have somebody check with anybody who might know where I might'a been the day of that day in time, would'ja?

THE VICE PRESIDENT. I believe what the president remembers is that we have already claimed that we've already passed that information on to the committee, Mister Pandergast.

PANDERGAST. Our records don't seem to have recorded that, sir.

THE VICE PRESIDENT. Fortunately for you, the White House keeps at least two sets of books on everything.

THE CHIEF ADVISOR. According to our daily log, that particular date frame in time happened to be a travel day for the president.

THE PRESIDENT. Travel's my chief way of gettin' aroun'. One thing I've learned is if I'm not here, it's a safe bet I'm somewhere else.

PANDERGAST. And in what place on that day did you find yourself other than actually being here, sir?

THE PRESIDENT. I think we were in New Mexico aroun' that time, weren't we, Manure Dumpling?

THE CHIEF ADVISOR. If we say we where we were, then that's where we were, it's as simple as that.

THE PRESIDENT. Was it New Mexico or was it Massachusetts? I know it was someplace with a "c" in it. I think it even started with a "see."

THE CHIEF ADVISOR. It was Secaucus, sir.

THE PRESIDENT. I knew it!

PANDERGAST. You were in New Jersey, sir?

THE PRESIDENT. Y'can't prove anything by me. All's I know is what they tell me was in the papers.

THE VICE PRESIDENT. We have footage of the event.

THE CHIEF ADVISOR. We have footage of every event.

THE VICE PRESIDENT. We have two sets of footage. At your particular question in time, Counselor, the president was being honored in Idaho at an international conference on illiteracy.

THE CHIEF ADVISOR. He was being honored for his lifelong dedication to keeping books on the front burner.

PANDERGAST. And it was there that you heard whatever it was that you heard, sir?

THE PRESIDENT. I must'a been if that's where I heard it.

THE CHIEF ADVISOR. The other truth is that because of the time difference, the president was fast asleep at the time that he didn't hear whatever it was that he didn't.

PANDERGAST. It was the middle of the night?

THE CHIEF ADVISOR. More like noon.

THE PRESIDENT. Cap'n Cat Nap, that's me. Had a working snooze on my bike the other day. Didn't slow me up a lick.

(drinks from his bottle, then)

Hard to believe, right? Me, drinkin' French water?

THE CHIEF ADVISOR. Perhaps you've had enough of it for now, sir.

THE PRESIDENT. I was never one fer bearin' a grudge, y'know? Fergiven's a whole lot more Christian-Judeeo, fergivin' is. It's a whole lot more Muslamic, too. That's my motto, y'know what I mean? Ya gotta jes' let bygones be – *(can't remember the word)* – Stuff that's jes' gone by.

PANDERGAST. And upon hearing the news of the total inundation of the entirety of the nation's capital, Mister President?

THE VICE PRESIDENT. The president immediately boarded Air Force One.

PANDERGAST. But in which he flew straight to Texas?

THE PRESIDENT. That baby can get there with its eyes shut.

THE CHIEF ADVISOR. The president had a longstanding commitment to speak at a black tie fund raiser and target practice dinner.

THE PRESIDENT. Should'a brought you along, Dickie.
(aside to **PANDERGAST***)* I like to razz him - make his pacemaker skip a beat every now and then.

PANDERGAST. So when then, in all factuality, Mister President, did you finally touch down in the capital after receiving first word of the life threatening as well as taking crisis there?

THE PRESIDENT. I'd say it was no more than - what does the team reckon, guys? Three, four – ?

THE VICE PRESIDENT. Closer to three.

THE PRESIDENT. Yeah. It was about three weeks later.

PANDERGAST. And to those who say that seemed an unseemly, even an obscenely, length of time, sir?

THE VICE PRESIDENT. The president is aware that there is a certain element in this country for whom nothing this president does or doesn't do is ever going to be what they think he should have done. And that extends to whatever he didn't do, which is more or less what they think he always does.

THE CHIEF ADVISOR. That's the same element who would have found fault if the president had taken two weeks to reach the scene of the disaster.

THE PRESIDENT. Y'can't let these things get too next t'ya, know what I mean? I'm just not interested in any negative that's not a positive.

THE VICE PRESIDENT. This is a wartime president who is at peace with himself.

THE PRESIDENT. I get my big shoulders from my mom.

THE VICE PRESIDENT. A check of our records will show that since the flood, the president has paid no less than twenty-seven visits to Washington, D.C.

THE CHIEF ADVISOR. The truth is, now that he's not there anymore, he's been there more times than he's ever been there before.

PANDERGAST. But you are aware, Mister President, I'm sure, of the depth of disgruntlement, especially among the refugees, who felt that your presence in the capitol at such a critical time in moment would have been a great deal more helpful than your absence proved to be?

THE PRESIDENT. *(His tongue just a bit thick now)* Let me finish.

PANDERGAST. You weren't saying anything, sir.

THE PRESIDENT. You sure?

THE VICE PRESIDENT. You were finished, Mister President.

THE PRESIDENT. I came to a period at the end?

THE CHIEF ADVISOR. Yes, sir.

THE PRESIDENT. Then how 'bout a little refill here, huh, Fecal Face?

THE CHIEF ADVISOR. Sir, I'm not sure you should –

THE VICE PRESIDENT. *(overlapping)* Maybe we'd better just –

THE CHIEF ADVISOR. *(overlapping)* What's the time getting to be?

PANDERGAST. *(overlapping)* Haven't I still got a few – ?

THE VOICE OVER. Unfortunately, AGN is unable to show its viewers the balance of the president's interview, due to a sudden, inexplicable power outage at the temporary White House, an outage which brought the taping to a complete stop. However, as one of our technicians was making his own back-up sound recording one we were able to later retrieve, we are now able to bring you the following audio portion of the balance of the president's testimony.

THE PRESIDENT. We all right here, boys? What happened there?

THE VICE PRESIDENT. We're fine, Mister President.

THE PRESIDENT. Why's the red light off?

THE VICE PRESIDENT. The interview's all over, sir.

THE PRESIDENT. It is? Wasn't I was sayin' somethin' before I stopped talkin'?

THE CHIEF ADVISOR. Actually, the counsel's time has run completely out, Mister President.

PANDERGAST. But if you like –

THE VICE PRESIDENT. The taping's over.

THE CHIEF ADVISOR. Over and a half.

THE PRESIDENT. Hey, I'm the one calls the shots around here. No offense, Dicky-bird. What were we talkin' about, Panderooney, you remember?

PANDERGAST. We were discussing the refugee situation, Mister President.

THE PRESIDENT. Stop right there, okay? I jes' hate that. Those people, those lawmakers, the ones TV showed evacuatin' all over town? Callin' 'em refugees was very hurtful of their feelings, y'know what I'm sayin'? It was insulting. We're not talkin' about a bunch'a filthy foreigners here. Those dirty, homeless, I hear even smelly, people were decent, hardworkin', tax spendin' public servants. My heart goes out big-time to them. 'An I think they know down deep in each one'a their own that I've already taken about as much human responsibility fer what happened to them as any one man can ever be told he should be takin'. Ya sure ya don' want a splash'a this?

PANDERGAST. No, thank you, sir.

THE PRESIDENT. Pooty sends me a case a week. His private stock. Good guy, Pooty. Looked into that man's eyes first time we met an' I saw his soul. Saw the man's soul right down to his galoshes.

THE VICE PRESIDENT. You may go now, Counselor.

THE CHIEF ADVISOR. That's a wrap.

PANDERGAST. But the president's still willing to –

THE CHIEF ADVISOR. Leave everything. Go.

THE VICE PRESIDENT. You can collect it all later.

THE PRESIDENT. Thing of it is, see, I'm gonna make everything right again. Gonna put the town back together. Gonna make D.C. a stronger, even freer country than it ever was before.

THE VICE PRESIDENT. Let's move on out, people.

THE CHIEF ADVISOR. Leave it all.

THE PRESIDENT. Washington's comin' back bigger'n ever. I'm already workin' on plans fer its embetterment.

What we're gonna do, we're gonna open casinos. This is one government that's finally gonna turn a profit. I know gambling's illegal in D.C., but did you know a president's allowed to disregard any law he feels like, as long as there's a war goin' on?An' I can have as many'a those as I feel like. Thing is, I din't get where I am 'cause I was elected, y'know. I was selected - picked out by faith and destiny and God only knows what else -picked out to advance the cause of liberty. An' there's not one single liberty I won't take carryin' the whole world with me right into the end zone. Who the hell was it said somethin' like that once before? Wonder if ole Mister 41's asleep?

(Sound: A receiver is lifted. During a phone tone.)

THE PRESIDENT. *(sings quietly)* "I'm an old cowhand…from the Rio Grande…"
(spoken) Hey! Popster?

(uses a squirt of Binaca for his breath)

No, no, not him. This is your bad boy.
(chuckles, then) Listen, who was it said whatever about extremism defending liberty bein' no vice? That moderation in the pursuit of virtue thingy? You remember?
(listens, then) Goldwater! Right! Bingo!
(listens, then) Man was bright as hell, wasn't he?
(listens, then) Really? He was only half Gentile? Hey, well, ya know what they always say - ya live an' ya - an' ya whatever.
(listens, then) How ya doin'? Have a good day?
(listens, then) An 85? No kiddin'?
(laughs) Was that fer nine holes or 18?
(listens, then) No kiddin' - ya stayed the whole course? Good fer you. I'll letcha go now. Give the Chief of staff a hug 'n a kiss.
(listens, then) No, no, no, don' put her on. I've been catchin' enough hell around here. No, don't!
(a beat; then, resigned) How ya doin'?

(listens, then) No, no, I never said I didn' wanna talk. I was checkin' somethin' out, an' he jes' happened ta picked up the phone.

(listens, then) My britches are not one size bigger.

(listens, then) No, ma'am. I haven't had a drop.

(listens, then) Hey, he's who he is, I'm who you made me. It's a helluva lot easier runnin' jes' one little ole state, y'know. I'd like ta see how good he'd be lookin' after, what is it? Mus' be fifty of 'em.

(listens, then) Cut me a little slack, can'cha once? Y'got 'ny idea all the crap keeps comin' down on my plate aroun' here? Y'got 'ny idea how many changes there've been aroun' here since you ran this place?

(listens, then) Yeah, but —

(listens a moment, then) Sorry.

(listens, then) I said I was sorry. Please finish. I won't. Go ahead.

(listens, then, with a sigh) Uh huh...right...right...

(His voice growing ever smaller, ever fainter.)

Right...right...right...

THE VOICE OVER. Feeling that nothing could adequately follow the words of the President of the United States in his very own words, it fell to the chairman of the committee to bring the hearings to a close with a dual pronouncement:

GROSS. God bless America. And God help us all.

(sound: gavel)

THE VOICE OVER. From AGN - where - just as sure as one Gate closes — another can't wait to swing open - we bid you good night.

(sound: gavel)

THE END

www.ingramcontent.com/pod-product-compliance
Lightning Source LLC
Chambersburg PA
CBHW070419120726
47909CB00005B/1719